© 2018 Viacom International Inc. All rights reserved. Nickelodeon, *The Loud House* and all related titles, logos and characters are trademarks of Viacom International Inc.

All rights reserved. Published by Scholastic Inc., *Publishers since 1920*. SCHOLASTIC and associated logos are trademarks and/or registered trademarks of Scholastic Inc.

ISBN 978-1-338-68152-9

10 9 8 7 6 5 4 3        20 21 22 23 24

Printed in the U.S.A.        40

Scholastic first edition 2020

# WHO GHOST THERE?

By Karla Sakas Shropshire

I stared at the clock, willing it to strike three. Thirty more seconds . . . twenty-nine . . . Is it just me, or do all classroom clocks seem to slow down at the end of the day? I glanced over at my best friend, Clyde. His eyes were glued to the clock, too, while his pen trailed off his worksheet and onto his desk. I was about to point this out when the clock finally struck three and the school bell rang.

"Yes!" I exclaimed, jumping out of my seat.

"Thank you for volunteering to clean out the gerbil cage, Lincoln! Love that enthusiasm," I heard Mrs. Johnson say. Wait, what? I glanced over to see my teacher standing by the class pet, Chompy. "Looks as if he went through two full water bottles today," she added.

*Whoops.* Guess I hadn't exactly been paying attention—but could you blame me? My mind was elsewhere, on my favorite TV show, the *Academy of Really Good Ghost Hunters!*—or as we ghost-hunting cadets called it, *ARGGH!* A brand-new episode was starting in thirty minutes, and Cadets Lincoln and Clyde weren't going to miss a single second.

Clyde raised his hand. "I'll help him!" he

said, before turning to me and whispering, "But why do you want to clean Chompy's cage? Shouldn't we get to my house so we can watch *ARGGH!*?"

I face-palmed. "Sorry, Clyde. My excitement got the better of me."

Cleaning the cage turned out to be a two-person job after all. I switched the cedar shavings while Clyde distracted Chompy with food so he wouldn't sink his little gerbil fangs into our fingers.

"Maybe using baby carrots wasn't the best idea," Clyde said, fifteen minutes later, as he watched me wrap a bandage around my hand. "Chompy must have mistaken your thumb for a carrot." I looked over at the gerbil, who smirked back from his now-clean cage.

"*Sure* he did. But never mind that—we have a show to catch. Let's go!" I said, grabbing my backpack and helmet. We darted out the front doors, hopped on our bikes and raced to Clyde's house. We always watch *ARGGH!* at Clyde's, not just because his dads make the best snacks, but also because he doesn't have to share a TV with ten sisters. Unlike me.

I'm Lincoln Loud, and yes, that's right. I have ten sisters—five older, five younger— which means it's almost impossible to get the TV to myself at home. Not just the TV, actually, but nearly everything: the last slice of pizza, the good spot on the couch, the few remaining drops of hot water before the shower turns icy—you get the idea. That's life in a big family for you. Still, I wouldn't trade it for anything. As chaotic as our household can get, my sisters are ten awesome and unique people I'm lucky to call family. Most days, anyway.

**C**lyde and I made it to his house with seconds to spare. His dads greeted us at the door with a big bowl of kettle corn and a plate of buffalo chicken sliders—I told you the snacks were good—and proceeded with their usual rapid-fire questions about Clyde's day.

"Hi, Clyde, how was school? Did you have

any trouble opening your new lunch bag?" his dad Harold said.

"Did your sinuses act up? Did you strain any muscles in gym?" asked his other dad, Howard.

Maybe you've heard of helicopter parents? Clyde's dads are more like a SWAT team fast-roping out of the chopper at the merest hint of danger.

"Sorry, but I'll have to fill you guys in later. There's a new episode of *ARGGH!* on," Clyde told them.

"Oh, of course," Harold said, handing us the snacks, then stepping aside. As much as his dads like to worry, they understand how important *ARGGH!* is to Clyde and me.

"Careful with the kettle corn," Howard called after us. "I checked for unpopped kernels, but there could still be one lurking in there. Don't want to crack a tooth!"

Clyde and I dashed into the living room and turned on the TV just as the opening credits for *ARGGH!* began to play. The show's logo flashed on the screen, then dissolved into shaky black-and-white footage of an old abandoned ice rink. Dim fluorescent lights flickered over rusty bleachers and a burned-out scoreboard. Distant drips echoed off the mildew-streaked walls. Everything was dingy and run-down except the ice, which was perfectly smooth and seemed to emit an eerie glow. Hunter Spector, the host of *ARGGH!,* stepped out of the shadows.

"Welcome back, *ARGGH!* cadets!" he said. "Tonight we're at an abandoned hockey rink in Ottawa, Canada, rumored to be haunted by the spirit of Ignacio, the angry ice keeper."

A blurry black-and-white photograph of Ignacio flashed on the screen. He *did* look angry.

Hunter went on. "Ignacio couldn't bear to see his perfect ice destroyed day in, day out. Every scratch from a hockey skate sliced right through his heart. People told him to change careers, to get into cake decorating or cement pouring instead. But Ignacio refused. And one day, in the middle of a particularly rough hockey match, he snapped."

Gritty reenactment footage flashed onto the screen. Clyde and I exchanged grins—we loved the reenactments! We watched as a crazy-eyed man in a knit cap drove one of those giant ice resurfacing machines straight into a pack of beefy hockey players, sending them flying.

Hunter continued gravely. "When they tried to take away the keys to his Zamboni, Ignacio just kept driving—straight out of the arena and into the night, never to be seen again. After that, no one ever played another hockey game on this ice. Something—or *someone*—has been keeping the players away."

He took out his EMF (electromagnetic field) detector and held it up to the camera. The needle hovered in the red zone. Hunter grinned.

"Looks like Ignacio's in the building. What say we . . . break the ice?" he quipped, before pulling a hockey mask down over his face and skating onto the rink.

Immediately, the lights went out in the arena,

leaving only the eerie glow of the ice. Clyde and I leaned closer to the TV, not wanting to miss a thing. Hunter skated across the rink, doing figure eights and reversals, the blades of his skates cutting through the ice. Suddenly, on the other side of the arena, a Zamboni roared to life. Clyde and I gasped as the hulking machine made its way toward Hunter, picking up speed.

"I think someone's headed for a meltdown," Hunter deadpanned, ripping open a bag of road salt and spraying it across the rink. The ice melted on contact, forming a giant pool in the middle of the arena. Unable to stop, the Zamboni drove straight into it, wheels whirring hopelessly as it tried to escape.

"And now to let him cool off!" Hunter shouted, throwing the switch on the arena's freezing unit. Within seconds, the ice had refrozen—with the Zamboni lodged firmly in it. The hulking machine gave one last feeble whirr before the engine died and the lights went out.

*Whoa.* Clyde and I sat back in the sofa. *One week later* flashed on-screen. The ice rink was back in business, with a hockey game in full swing. The players skated deftly around the Zamboni, which sat silently in the middle of the rink. Ignacio's angry spirit had clearly abandoned it. I turned to Clyde, whose mouth was hanging open in awe.

"Okay, I know we usually have a formal vote, but this definitely belongs on our list of all-time favorite episodes," I said.

"Definitely," Clyde agreed. On TV, Hunter looked directly into the camera.

"Before I sign off tonight, I have a special announcement for my *ARGGH!* cadets," he said. Clyde and I shot to attention.

"You guys watch me hunt ghosts every week; now I want to see *you* in action! Send in your videos of paranormal activity, to be featured in our new Cadet Spotlight at the end of every show!"

Clyde and I looked at each other, psyched. This was our chance to prove ourselves as *ARGGH!* cadets and show our fearless leader, Hunter Spector, that we'd absorbed everything he'd taught us. The only problem was, we'd never captured a ghost on video before. In fact, I wasn't even sure where to start looking for one.

Back on-screen, Hunter Spector continued. "Remember, cadets, paranormal activity can be found lurking anywhere—hockey rinks, theme parks, gas stations—even in your own homes!"

Of course! I beamed at Clyde, who frowned, looking around his impeccably decorated living room.

"Sorry, Lincoln, but I don't think there are any ghosts here. My dads just renovated, and we probably would have found them when they pulled out all that old shag carpeting."

I shook my head. "Actually, I was thinking about my house. It's *really* old. And creaky. And it hasn't been renovated in years—apart from the time Lori and Leni tried to turn my bedroom into a walk-in closet. There's bound to be a ghost creeping around somewhere!"

Clyde shot up, sending the bowl of kettle corn flying. "What are we waiting for?" he said. "Let's go!"

Just then, Clyde's dads came running into the room.

"Are you boys okay? I thought I heard kernels flying! Oh, Harold, I knew we should have stuck to pudding!"

**C**lyde and I suited up in our official *ARGGH!* cadet gear: *ARGGH!* jumpsuits, *ARGGH!* EMF detectors, *ARGGH!* walkie-talkies, and *ARGGH!* night-vision goggles. The goggles don't technically work—that'd be asking a lot for $19.95—but they complete the look. Then we charged the battery on our video camera, hopped on our bikes, and set off for my house.

The sun was starting to set, casting eerie shadows across our neighborhood. The evening air was chilly, and we could see our breath as we pedaled.

"Is it just me, or is this the perfect night for ghost hunting?" Clyde asked.

"You read my mind, Cadet Clyde!" I called back, grinning. "Should we review our ghost-hunting protocol?"

Years of watching Hunter Spector at work had taught us a thing or two about spotting signs of paranormal activity. First and foremost, we'd have our trusty EMF detectors on hand, ready to read any unusually high concentrations of electromagnetic energy—the telltale mark of ghostly entities. But we'd also be on the lookout for sudden changes in temperature, disturbances in electrical devices, hot and cold air currents, unusual behavior in animals, levitating objects, unexplained sounds, and— if we were *really* lucky—the holy grail of ghost hunting: floating orbs.

We pulled into my driveway at the same time that my mom and dad came out the front door. I caught a whiff of fancy perfume and aftershave.

"Hey, Mom and Dad! Date night?" I said as Clyde and I jumped off our bikes. My mom smiled.

"That's right. Your dad and I are headed to couples' karaoke night at Jean Juan's French-Mex Buffet," she said. My dad checked his watch just as their taxi pulled up.

"Hi, boys. I'd love to stay and chat, but if we don't put our names on the list early, another couple might take all the good songs," he said anxiously, getting in the back of the cab.

"Is it cool if Clyde hangs out for a little while?" I asked as my mom got in the taxi, too.

"Of course! Just remember, Lori's in charge," she said. Then the car took off. Behind me, Clyde started stammering.

"L-L-Lori?"

I turned. Clyde practically had hearts in his eyes. He's got a huge crush on my oldest sister. He can't even be in the same room with her without passing out. I tried to get his attention.

"Clyde? Clyde?" Nothing. I sighed and hit the call button on my *ARGGH!* walkie-talkie. Clyde's walkie went off, jolting him back to reality.

"Sorry, Lincoln. I was just thinking about how beautiful Lori's eyelashes are," he said, before quickly adding, "So where do you think we should start our search?"

I glanced at the house. Through the living-room window, I could see Lori pacing back and forth, waving her phone around in search of better cell reception. Okay, definitely not there. Before Clyde could spot her, I steered him over to the side of the house.

"Why don't we start with the basement? Then we can work our way up, doing a sweep of each floor," I suggested.

Clyde nodded. "That sounds just like what Hunter would say," he said. "Remember the time he tracked the spirit of the furious furnace tender?"

How could I forget? It's on our list of all-time favorite *ARGGH!* episodes. Though to be fair, it's one of fifty.

Clyde and I stopped in front of the storm doors to the basement.

"You ready to do this, Cadet Clyde?" I asked.

"You know it, Cadet Lincoln," Clyde said, grinning. He held up the video camera and pressed record. We pulled down our night-vision goggles. Then, remembering that the goggles don't actually work, we pulled them back up and stepped down into the darkness.

**C**lyde and I slowly descended the stairs into the shadowy basement. The pipes dripped in the brisk air, and a shiver ran down my spine. It was like walking straight into an episode of *ARGGH!* I turned and whispered to Clyde.

"Okay, let's listen for any disturbances, even the slightest sound—"

*CLANG! CLANG!* Two loud blasts rang out through the basement. Caught off guard, I tripped over the bottom step. Clyde bumped into me, and we both tumbled to the floor.

"Gah! The video camera!" Clyde yelped as it flew through the air. A hand reached out to grab it just in time.

"Boom! Reflexes!" a familiar voice shouted. I looked up to see my sister Lynn, the thirteen-year-old sports fanatic, grinning down at us in the dim light. She was wearing workout gear and clutching our video camera in one hand. She easily pulled Clyde to his feet, then handed him back the camera.

"Now if you guys don't mind, I'll return to my workout. I just crushed a protein shake and I'm ready to hit some new personal bests," she said, jerking a thumb toward a weight machine.

I stepped forward. "Actually, Lynn, we were hoping to do some paranormal investigating down here. Any chance you could clear out for a few?" I asked in my politest voice, adding, "Ghosts don't really come out when weights are clanging around."

Lynn frowned and mimicked the sound of a sports buzzer. "*EHHH!* No way. I was just getting into the zone," she said, returning to the weight machine and pulling down on a bar, lifting a heavy stack of weights. Clyde watched, impressed.

"Wow, Lynn, I didn't know you were that strong," he said.

"It's just a warm-up," she huffed. "You guys want to do a push-up challenge when I'm done with this set?" Lynn never passed up an opportunity to work out—or to compete.

"Uh, maybe next time," I said, before turning to Clyde. "Come on, buddy. There's no use expecting ghosts to show up with all this racket. Let's try upstairs in the kitchen."

Clyde lit up. "Good idea! Remember that episode where Hunter tracked down the spirit of the angry sous chef?"

Of course I did! Another one of our top-fifty classics. Hunter had found the ghost lurking inside an old walk-in refrigerator and drove it out with an eggbeater. Simple but genius.

As Clyde and I climbed the stairs to my kitchen, I wondered if there was a ghost in *our*

refrigerator. With so many layers of ancient leftovers, it's been years since anyone's seen the back of it.

"The other day, I was looking for milk and I found a piece of my old birthday cake—from when I turned six!" I told Clyde. "Who knows what else might be in there."

We pushed open the door to the kitchen, only to find my baby sister, Lily, parked in front of the refrigerator. She was concentrating very hard on arranging the alphabet magnets into nonsense words. Adorable, but we really needed to get in there.

"Don't worry, I'll just scoot her out of the way," I assured Clyde. I heard someone clear her throat and looked over to see my sister Lisa, the four-year-old genius, sitting at the kitchen table. She was in her usual lab coat and safety goggles, surrounded by chemicals and stirring a beaker of sticky green goo.

"I would advise against attempting to relocate our youngest sibling. She is in a rather cantankerous mood today," Lisa said flatly, without looking up from her work. "I attempted to enlist her assistance in a harmless test of my new super-strength adhesive and was rewarded with a bite on the forearm." She held up her arm to show us. Clyde and I winced.

Lily might have only one tooth, but she wields it like a mighty sword. Between that and her penchant for going to the bathroom wherever she likes, Lily and Chompy have a lot in common. At least I knew better than to try to distract her with baby carrots. I turned to Lisa.

"Well, unlike you, *I'm* not trying to trick

her into being my test subject," I replied. "I'm just trying to check the fridge for paranormal activity."

"There could be the spirit of an angry sous chef in there!" Clyde added, excited.

Lisa blinked at us. "As a woman of science, I refuse to dignify those statements with a response." Ignoring her, I crouched down and smiled at Lily, who was babbling to herself as she banged two magnets together.

"Hey, Lilster. Think we could just scoot you over this way for a sec?" I asked, starting to pick her up.

Lily's eyes scrunched up. Oh no. I knew what was coming, but it was too late. She wriggled out of my grasp and threw herself against the fridge, bursting into an angry wail. Behind us,

Lisa sighed to herself.

"Sorrysorrysorrysorry, Lily! Our mistake!" I said quickly, backing away from the fridge. She blew an angry raspberry at Clyde and me, then sniffled and returned to playing with her magnets. Within seconds, she was happily babbling to herself again. Well, at least there was no lasting damage.

"Come on, Clyde, let's go. Any ghosts that might have been in there were probably scared off by Lily's incredibly loud wail." Lisa scoffed. I ignored her and turned to Clyde, who suggested we try the dining room next.

"We have an old grandfather clock with some serious spooky potential," I said. Clyde's eyes widened.

"Ooh, just like when Hunter tracked the

spirit of the cuckoo cuckoo-clock maker!"
Clyde said.

"Exactly!" I replied. We headed into the
dining room, video camera rolling.

Instead of a haunted grandfather clock, however, we found another one of my sisters—and about twenty dolls and stuffed animals. Lola, the glitter-loving half of the six-year-old twins, informed us that she was holding a pageant for her toys. She was wearing a sash with *Judge* spelled out in sequins.

"Would you two like to be guest judges? You're just in time for the talent portion!" she exclaimed as one of her animatronic stuffed bears danced jerkily across the dining-room table. This was ridiculous. I wasn't going to let our paranormal investigations be thwarted by a dancing bear.

"Sure, we'll judge," I said, grabbing the clipboard.

"Gosh, Lincoln, do you really think we're qualified?" Clyde asked.

"Just go with it," I muttered, then drew a big number ten on the score sheet and held it up for Lola. "I think Mr. Sprinkles is the clear winner—look at that fancy footwork! Ten out of ten, pageant's over. How about you retire to the kitchen for the after-party?"

Lola's face instantly transformed from a sweet smile to a stony glare. It's unnerving how she can do that.

"Are you kidding?" she asked incredulously, her eyes flashing with anger. "We haven't even gotten to the eveningwear competition! I was up *all night* sewing their gowns."

Clyde and I took a step back, alarmed. I knew better than to get into it with her. One time, I'd asked her to relocate her hopscotch grid so Clyde and I could set up a bike ramp in the driveway. She wasn't even using it! But the next day, both of my bike tires had been slashed—and there were traces of glitter on the wheel spokes.

"Come on, Clyde," I said. "Maybe we'll have better luck in the living room. I heard some weird noises coming from the chimney last week. It could have been that possum again, but it also could have been—"

"—the spirit of a lonely chimney sweep, just like the one Hunter found!" Clyde chimed in. I grinned and headed into the living room—only to be knocked off my feet.

*OOF!* I looked up to see Lana, the mud-loving half of the six-year-old twins, bounding away on all fours. I stood up.

"Lana, what the—?" I started to say, but then—*OOF!*—I was knocked down again, this time by our bulldog, Charles. As Clyde pulled me to my feet, I saw that the living room had been converted into a homemade dog agility course. Clyde and I watched, confused, as Lana plowed over a set of hurdles, crawled through a tunnel, jumped across a seesaw, and bounded through a hoop with Charles following close behind. As they crossed the finish line, Lana stood up and clicked a stopwatch.

"One minute, ten seconds," she said to Charles. "Not bad, but let's see if we can get over those hurdles a little faster." She handed him a treat, then turned to Clyde and me while Charles chowed down.

"Sorry about that, Lincoln," she said. "But I couldn't stop in the middle of a run—Charles and I are training for an agility competition."

"The humans have to go through the course, too?" Clyde asked, confused.

Lana shook her head. "I *wish*! But nah, I'm just showing Charles how to do the obstacles. It's how he learns best. Well, that and lots of treats."

There had to be a way to get Lana and

Charles to leave. I glanced out the window, then back at Lana. "This is a pretty sweet course," I said. "But couldn't you make an even better one in the yard? You could use the baby pool as a water obstacle!"

Lana shook her head. "No can do. Lucy's out there grave-digging. Didn't want to risk falling into one and twisting a paw, did we, boy?" she said, looking down at Charles, who was trying to pull the bag of treats out of her pocket. She handed him one, then sneaked another for herself.

"Lana! Mom and Dad said you aren't supposed to eat Charles's treats anymore," I said. Lana growled at me. Charles looked up at her, then started growling at me, too. I guess that really is how he learns best. I sighed.

"So much for investigating the chimney,"

I said to Clyde. I was starting to get a bad feeling about this ghost hunt—were my sisters really going to turn up everywhere Clyde and I went? There had to be *some*place they hadn't infiltrated. Clyde seemed to be thinking the same thing.

"We're not having much luck on the first floor, are we? Should we try upstairs?"

I looked around, thinking for a second.

"I've got a better idea! Why don't we try somewhere in between. . . ."

**C**lyde and I peered into the air vent.

"Good thinking, Lincoln. It's just like when Hunter was tracking the ghost of the angry AC repairwoman!" Clyde exclaimed.

"Exactly! You know, sometimes I do hear strange sounds coming from the vents," I said as we took off the grate and climbed inside. We crawled forward and were soon swallowed up in the darkness.

"It's times like these I really wish we had sprung for the real night-vision gogg— GAH!" I yelped as I bumped into something solid in front of me.

"Is it a ghost?" Clyde asked optimistically, scrambling to turn on the video camera.

"Sigh. If only," came a monotone reply. I knew that monotone.

"Lucy?" I asked into the darkness. As my eyes adjusted, I saw her sitting cross-legged in the vents, her pet bat, Fangs, on her shoulder. Fangs squeaked at us. Lucy stared at us. Or at least, I think she did. Her bangs covered her eyes.

"What are you doing in here? Lana said you were outside digging graves," I said.

"Sigh. I was—until I hit the gas line and was forced to abandon my work. Mom and Dad have zero appreciation for the mortuary arts," Lucy replied, then held up a black notebook and pen. "So I came in here to vent."

I know that sounds like a joke, but trust me when I say she's not the type.

"This is where I always come to express my inner torment," Lucy said. Guess that explained the strange sounds I'd heard coming from the vents before. Clyde tapped my shoulder.

"We should probably leave her in peace. Dr. Lopez says journaling can be a positive outlet for negative emotions," he said, referring to his therapist. "And it can serve as inspiration for our creative endeavors." Then he turned to Lucy. "I hope your torment turns into your best poem yet!"

For a second, I could have sworn I saw Lucy break into a smile. But then Fangs flapped off her shoulder and flew straight at me.

"Okay, okay, I can take a hint! We're leaving!" I said, scooting backward with my hands over my neck, just to be safe.

Back outside, Clyde and I regrouped. We'd searched more than half of the house without finding a single trace of paranormal activity— all thanks to my ever-present sisters.

"Maybe we should try upstairs after all— say, starting with Lori's room?" Clyde suggested hopefully.

"No way, Clyde. I know better than to snoop in my sisters' bedrooms . . . unless we want to become ghosts ourselves," I said.

There was always *my* room. My kingdom. My domain. True, it's just a converted linen closet, but I'm pretty lucky to be the only Loud kid with a room to myself. Or at least, I'd always *assumed* I had the place to myself. If there was even a slight chance that I had a ghostly roommate, now was the time to find out.

Clyde and I climbed the stairs and peered into the upstairs hall. All the bedroom doors were closed, and there wasn't a sister in sight. I couldn't believe our luck.

"Wow," I whispered to Clyde. "It's never this quiet. Maybe our ghost hunt is finally about to pick up!" He flashed me an enthusiastic thumbs-up, and together we crept down the hall toward my room. Clyde got out the video camera; then I slowly pushed open the door.

Dark shadows fell across my bedroom. My clock ticked ominously. Clyde and I stepped into the darkness, holding our breath. Suddenly, a jarring voice rang out behind me. We both jumped.

"Say, what do you call two bananas?" it squawked. Clyde and I turned to see my sister Luan the comedian holding her ventriloquist dummy, Mr. Coconuts.

Luan stared at her dummy, feigning cluelessness. "Gee, I don't know, Mr. Coconuts, what *do* you call them?"

"A pair of slippers. Get it?" Mr. Coconuts replied, before Luan burst into her trademark giggle. Clyde laughed and clapped.

"Good one, Mr. Coconuts!" he said. Luan smiled and made the dummy take a bow.

"If you found that joke a-*peeling,* we've got *bunches* more to tell before you *split,*" Mr. Coconuts gabbled. "Like this one: What did the banana say to the monkey?"

Clyde furrowed his brow, thinking. I sighed.

"We don't have time for your ventriloquist act right now, Luan. Clyde and I are in the middle of a ghost hunt."

Mr. Coconuts glared at me. "Yeah, well, I'm in the middle of a joke, pal! And you just stepped on my punch line!"

I pleaded with Luan. "Look, we can't hunt for ghosts if it's not quiet. Can't you just work on your mime act instead?" Mr. Coconuts's mouth fell open, probably to deliver a searing comedic retort, when—*BLANGGG!*—an earsplitting power chord rang out in the hallway. There was no need to ask where it came from.

"Luna!" Luan, Clyde, and I all said at once. I stormed into the hall, Clyde right behind me, and knocked loudly on my third-oldest sister's door. Luna stopped playing for a second and knocked back in a rhythmic pattern. I frowned.

"Not in the mood right now, Luna. Just open the door!" I shouted. The door opened and Luna leaned out, her electric guitar slung around her neck.

"'Sup, li'l dudes? I'm just taking my new whammy bar for a spin. Wanna come jam?" she asked.

Sometimes I understand only half of what Luna says, but it's usually safe to assume it involves some kind of song lyric or musical equipment. Clyde stepped forward.

"I'd love to jam! Do you have a recorder I could borrow? We just learned *'Frère Jacques'* in music class," he said eagerly. Luna grinned and waved Clyde inside, but I pulled him back, getting frustrated.

"Luna, we're not here to jam—we're here to look for ghosts! So will you please quit playing for a minute?" I asked. She shook her head.

"Dude, asking me to quit playing is like asking me to quit breathing," she replied.

Geez, dramatic much? Usually Luna's the chill, easygoing type. In fact, that gave me an idea.

"How about changing things up and going acoustic?" I tried. Luna paused to consider.

"Hmm, the mellow vibe. I can dig it," she said, putting down her electric guitar. Clyde and I exchanged surprised grins—finally, some progress! But just as she picked up her acoustic guitar, we heard a roar from inside the bathroom. What now?

I turned and rapped angrily on the bathroom door. My second-oldest sister, Leni, poked her head out, blow-dryer in hand. The tiled bathroom walls were amplifying the sound.

"Oh, hey, guys. Did you want me to style your hair next?" she asked. "I've always thought you'd look good with a fauxhawk, Lincoln."

I sighed. Of all my sisters, Leni is by far the sweetest—but my patience was wearing thin.

"No, we need you to turn the blow-dryer off. Can't you just let your hair . . . I don't know, dry by itself?"

Leni laughed. "And look like a total frizz ball? I thought Luan's doll was funny, but you, Lincoln, are hilarious!"

Before I could stop her, she ducked back into the bathroom—just as we heard Luna strike up another electrified chord in her room. Guess the mellow vibe didn't stick. Between Luan's comedy, Luna's music, and Leni's hair regimen, there was no hope of continuing our ghost hunt on the second floor. I was starting to feel desperate—we were running out of places to search. But then it hit me. As Lori would say, literally. I walked straight into the pull cord for the attic trapdoor.

"Clyde, there's still one place we haven't looked!" I exclaimed, pointing upward.

"The attic! Of course!" Clyde said. "It'll be just like when Hunter tracked the ghost of the angry old hermit. Or the ornery exterminator. Or the disgruntled insulation installer!" As Clyde ticked off seven more classic episodes of *ARGGH!* that featured attics, it occurred to me that maybe we should have started there in the first place.

Together, Clyde and I pulled open the trapdoor and peered up the stairs into the attic. Dust motes floated in the dim light. We got out the video camera and started climbing.

"This is our last chance," I said gravely. "If we don't find any paranormal activity up here, we aren't going to find it anywhere in my house."

Just then, we heard a deafening shriek.

Clyde and I dashed to the top of the attic steps and looked around wildly, trying to adjust our eyes to the darkness. My sister Lori came into view, pacing back and forth across the attic, talking on her cell phone.

"OMG, she did not! She did *not*!" Lori exclaimed, clearly in the middle of another gossip session with her friends. Behind me, I heard Clyde start to stutter. Oh no.

"L-L-L-Lori?" he said, growing faint. I grabbed him just as he passed out and set him down gently on the attic floor. Lori, oblivious, continued pacing with her phone, completely engrossed in her conversation.

"Chinah, this is too juicy, I can't even!" she squealed. I dug into a nearby dress-up trunk, pulled out a fan, and waved it over Clyde's face to try to rouse him.

"Hey, Lori?" I said, attempting to get her attention. "Lori? *LORI!*" I shouted. She finally looked over, irritated.

"Lincoln? What are you doing up here?"

I gritted my teeth and explained that we were trying to ghost hunt. "So do you think maybe you could take your phone call elsewhere? Or, I don't know, try a group text?" I begged. Lori looked at me as if I were crazy.

"This is literally the only place in the house I get reception," she said, before adding, "Now get out. This gossip is top-secret!"

Clyde was starting to come to. Before he could spot Lori again, I quickly put the night-vision goggles over his eyes and pulled him toward the attic steps.

**B**ack in my room, I flopped down on my bed in defeat. Clyde slumped in my desk chair, equally discouraged.

"Let's face it, Clyde," I groaned into my pillow. "We're never going to be able to find a ghost with all my sisters running around the house."

He nodded sadly. "Maybe we could try my nana's retirement condo instead. Everyone there is *really* quiet."

"That's a good idea, but I don't want to bug your nana. Besides, it's the principle of the thing," I said, sitting up. "This is my house, too! Just once I'd like to be able to do what I want without ten sisters getting in the way."

Clyde looked sympathetic, even though I knew this was outside only-child territory. He's a great friend like that.

"I'm not ready to give up on our paranormal investigations yet," I said. "If we can just get my sisters out of the house, I'm *positive* we'll find something spooky."

"But what would lure all of them out of the house? Your sisters are so different from each other," he pointed out.

"True . . . ," I began slowly. "But there has to be something they all have in common." *Apart from an uncommon talent for driving me crazy,* I thought.

Clyde and I racked our brains for somewhere to send my sisters. Not the mall—Lana, Lynn, and Lisa couldn't care less about shopping. Not Burpin' Burger—Lori was on another one of her health-food kicks. Not the movies, since our entire family was on a thirty-day ban after Lily somehow crawled inside the popcorn machine—sans diaper.

"Dairyland!" It's my family's favorite a-*moos*-ment park! Every one of my sisters is a huge fan.

Clyde looked impressed. "Wow, Lincoln. Did you get a raise in your allowance?" Good point. There was no way I could afford ten passes to Dairyland.

"Wait a minute," I said, getting an idea. "What if my sisters just *thought* they were going to Dairyland?"

Clyde looked confused. I went on, trying to piece together a plan.

"We could tell them there's a giveaway at Flip's Food and Fuel, and that the first ten people to say the magic word get free passes to Dairyland. That would get them out of the house in a heartbeat!"

Clyde frowned. "But that would be a lie, wouldn't it? What happens when they get to Flip's and there's no giveaway?" Admittedly, I hadn't quite worked out that part yet.

"Okay, so they'll probably be a little mad, but that's nothing I haven't handled before! The important thing is, while they're off at Flip's, we'll have the whole house to ourselves. Think of all the ghost hunting we could do!" Clyde still looked unsure. I pointed to the official *ARGGH!* logo on my jumpsuit. "Come on, what kind of cadets would we be if we didn't at least try?"

Clyde sighed. "Okay, but you have to be the one to tell them—I can't lie to my future bride."

**9**

"**F**ree passes to Dairyland? Like, completely free?" Lori asked skeptically. My sisters surrounded me in the living room, looking dubiously at the homemade flyer I'd just shown them. Clyde hid in the dining room, avoiding Lori's gaze.

"That's right," I said brightly. "All you have

to do is go up to the counter and say the magic word: *moo.*"

"Why aren't *you* going, Lincoln?" Lola asked, eyes narrowed. "You love Dairyland just as much as we do." I tried to look innocent.

"Yeah," Lynn chimed in. "Remember the time you rode the Curdler over and over until you puked?"

Lana got a dreamy look in her eyes, reminiscing. "The barf went *everywhere!*"

"Yeah, well, I'm glad you all remember that so vividly," I said.

"We took pictures!" Luan cried, getting out her phone. "Here, one's actually my lock screen right now—"

"Look," I interrupted. "There aren't enough free passes for Clyde and me to go, too, so we figured you guys should have them. For, you know . . . all the hard work you've been doing lately."

Lola's suspicious look transformed into a sugary smile.

"Aw, thanks, Linky! I *have* been working extra hard lately. Coordinating pageant attire for six different dolls is no easy task."

Lynn jumped up and punched the air a few times.

"What are we standing around here for? Let's grab those passes before someone else beats us to them. Dairyland! Dairyland!" she chanted. The rest of my sisters joined in, chanting as they headed for the front door.

I flashed a thumbs-up to Clyde, who was peeking out of the dining room—my plan had worked! He ducked as Lori ran back past him.

"Just one sec, I gotta grab my keys!" she

said, dashing up the stairs. Leni ran after her.

"Ooh, and I have to change into a Dairyland-themed outfit!" Leni cried.

"Ugh, and I gotta change this rancid diaper," Luna added. In typical Loud family fashion, everyone seemed to have something to take care of before leaving the house. I stood by the front door, trying to be patient, until finally, the last of my sisters filed outside.

"Are you sure you don't want to come, Lincoln?" asked Leni, now wearing a black-and-white cow-print skirt and little milkshake earrings.

"Nope. Those passes are all yours!" I grinned. Then I closed the door and turned to Clyde.

"And this house is all *ours*!" I cried. It was time for the real ghost hunt to begin.

**C**lyde and I headed for the basement again, restarting our sweep of the house. I couldn't get over how quiet it was. Even at night, I'd never heard my house this silent. The kitchen floor creaked as we tiptoed across it. The sound echoed through the empty house, giving me chills. I turned on the video camera.

"We should probably keep the camera rolling. In conditions like these, we need to be prepared for a spirit to make its presence known at any time," I said, thinking back to our *ARGGH!* ghost-hunting protocol.

I reached for the basement door, preparing to descend. Just then, we heard a faint, strange noise—but it wasn't coming from downstairs. It sounded much closer. Clyde and I strained our ears, listening to the odd scraping and squelching. It seemed to be coming from the living room. I waved for Clyde to follow me.

We crept through the dining room, then across the foyer and into the darkened living room. The noise was much louder in here. It was coming from the chimney.

Clyde grabbed me by the arm and started pantomiming a chimney sweep's dance.

I grinned and nodded. We crept up to the fireplace and peered inside it.

A sliver of moonlight filtered down through the chimney, illuminating the brick walls. But even though we could still hear the odd sounds, there was nothing there.

"What the heck?" I whispered to Clyde as I took out my EMF detector. The needle was hovering between the two highest levels. I showed Clyde. Something paranormal was definitely afoot. Clyde held up a hand.

"Wait a minute. . . . The sounds are moving," he whispered, pointing upward. Clyde was right. Whatever—or *whoever*—was inside the chimney was headed upstairs.

"Come on, let's go!" I whispered back. We made a beeline for the staircase. Whatever these spirits were, I didn't want to lose track of them.

What if they shook us off on the second floor?

Upstairs in the hallway, we heard a loud rattle coming from the attic. The pull cord on the trapdoor danced and shook, almost as if it were calling to us. As we crept closer, the EMF reader went nuts, the needle straining past the highest level. I showed Clyde, whose eyes widened. We were about to find ourselves an actual, live—well, technically not *live*—ghost. The rattling grew louder as I reached for the trembling pull cord.

"You ready to do this, Cadet Clyde? For real this time?" I asked. Clyde nodded, looking nervous but determined.

"Lead the way, Cadet Lincoln," he said, hoisting the video camera onto his shoulder.

My heart pounding, I pulled down the attic stairs and began to climb.

The attic was dark, but I could just make out a strange shape moving in the back corner. As my eyes adjusted, I realized the old dress-up trunk was rattling. There was something inside it. My stomach twisted into knots, but this was no time for an *ARGGH!* cadet to hesitate. I mustered my courage and yelled.

"Spirits, show yourselves!"

The trunk stopped rattling. I glanced back at Clyde, who was filming every second.

"Come on, let's go investigate," I said, taking a step toward the trunk. But just as I did, a stream of cold air rippled across the back of my neck. I jumped. So did Clyde.

"Whoa, did you feel that?" he said, clutching his neck.

"The spirits are on the move!" I exclaimed, looking wildly around the darkened attic. There was a loud creak behind us. I turned and couldn't believe my eyes. A massive old wooden wardrobe was rising slowly off the ground. It loomed over Clyde and me, creaking and swaying ominously.

"Whoever you are, state your business!" I shouted, trying to sound braver than I felt.

SLAM! The wardrobe crashed to the floor. The doors fell open, and something came floating out. Clyde and I gasped. We dashed forward to get a better look at the . . .

"Party balloons?" Clyde asked, confused, as we stared at the brightly colored decorations floating up to the ceiling. Before I could reply, music began to play. I looked around for the source, but it wasn't coming from a radio or a stereo. In fact, it didn't sound like any music I'd ever heard before—it was an eerie, otherworldly tune that was actually kind of catchy. The attic lights began flickering to the beat; then the wardrobe rose back off the floor, dancing and swaying along to the music. Behind us, the trunk joined in, rattling and spitting out scarves and boas in time with the music. My fear evaporated as I realized what the spirits were up to. I turned to Clyde, who was spinning around with the video camera, trying to capture everything.

"I think these spirits are here to party," I said.

Clyde grinned. "Hey, we should give them an intro, like Hunter does on *ARGGH!*," he said, flipping the camera around.

I nervously flattened down my cowlick and tried to channel Hunter's screen presence. No pressure.

"Hey, *ARGGH!* fans. Cadets Lincoln Loud and Clyde McBride here! We're in an attic in Royal Woods, Michigan, with . . . uh . . ."

"Well, we don't know what kind of spirits these are, but they know how to have a good time!" Clyde finished. As if in response, the music got louder and the wardrobe flapped its doors open and shut. Clyde turned the camera back around to get a close-up of it.

"Wait till Hunter sees this! Actually, wait till *everyone* sees this—on TV! You guys are going to be famous!" Clyde called out to the spirits. The lights flickered happily in response.

As I watched, awestruck, I couldn't help wondering who these spirits were. Had they always lived in my house and just never shown themselves before? They seemed so happy and good-natured. Had they been wanting to hang out this whole time?

I was about to ask when everything went quiet. The music fizzled out, the lights stopped flickering, the wardrobe returned to the floor, and the trunk stopped rattling.

"Wait, come back!" I shouted. But there was

no response. Clyde looked at me, perplexed.

"What do you think made them leave so quickly?" he asked.

Without warning, the front door to the house slammed. My sisters were back, their shouts filling the once-silent house.

"Of *course*." I sighed. Then I called out to the spirits again, hoping they could still hear me, even if they weren't going to show themselves. "Don't worry, guys, I get it. I can't blame you for wanting to hit the road now that my sisters are back. But don't feel like you have to. You should stick around—this is your house, too!"

Clyde and I headed for the attic stairs, amazed by what we'd just experienced.

"I'm not sure I'd believe it myself, if we didn't have it all on video," Clyde said. "Do you think we should add some title cards, like how they do it on *ARGGH!*? Or should we just send in the raw footage? This video's so good, it doesn't need any bells and whistles."

I was just as eager to send in our video, but I told Clyde that there was something I had to deal with first: the ten girls downstairs who'd just found out there were no free passes to Dairyland.

"Need backup?" he asked.

"I appreciate the offer, but you shouldn't risk it. If they turn me into a human pretzel, someone still has to make sure the video gets to *ARGGH!*"

Clyde nodded solemnly, then made a swift exit out the back door. I took a deep breath and headed to the living room to face my siblings. I know I said that ten angry sisters are nothing

I can't handle, but the prospect was starting to look a whole lot scarier than an attic full of ghosts.

I put on my most apologetic face. "Guys, I'm such an idiot. I mixed up the dates for the Dairyland giveaway! And then I couldn't find my phone to call you and—"

I stopped in my tracks, confused. To my shock, my sisters didn't look upset. In fact, they looked pleased. Lynn slugged me in the arm.

"Doesn't matter! Flip didn't know anything about Dairyland passes—but he *was* giving away free samples of his new Flippee flavor. Caramel apple!" she said, crushing an empty Flippee cup against her forehead.

"Highly recommend it," Lana said, letting out a loud belch.

"We would've gotten you one, too, Linky,

but they were for in-store customers only," Lola added sweetly. I fought back a grin, trying to look disappointed.

"Aw, man," I groaned. "Well, I'm glad you guys got something out of the trip, anyway."

Just then, Mom and Dad returned home from couples' karaoke night. Dad staggered through the front door, clutching his throat.

"Tea. With honey," he gasped before stumbling off toward the kitchen. Mom came in the door behind him, grinning.

"Hi, kids. How did everything go while your father and I were off"—she reached into her handbag and pulled out a plastic trophy of a microphone—"winning the golden mic!"

"Go, Mom and Dad!" we cheered. From the kitchen, we heard Dad rasp a feeble "thanks" and something about suffering for his art.

"Everything went great here," Lori said to Mom. "Thanks to Lincoln, we got free Flippees!" The other girls nodded in agreement. Mom smiled.

"What a good brother! I'm so proud of how kind you kids are to each other," she said, tousling my hair before heading to the kitchen.

I felt a pang of guilt. I *hadn't* been a good brother—I'd lied to my sisters. I was just lucky Flip chose today to be generous with his Flippees!

Later that night, as I brushed my teeth and got into bed, I still felt guilty, but I tried to push the feeling aside. Our video was incredible. We hadn't just found ghosts—we'd befriended them! Hunter was going to be so impressed. After all, most of the spirits he encountered were angry, and he had to drive them out. Maybe he'd even want to come to my house to meet these friendly spirits for himself. Of course, I wasn't sure how I'd get my sisters out of the way for *that.* It might require some real Dairyland tickets, which would require some serious saving.

I got into bed and pulled up the covers. Even though it was past half our bedtimes, the house was still full of noise. Lana was snoring, while Lola yelled at her to stop. Lily was crying, and Lisa was blasting her white-noise machine to drown it out. Luna was sleep-singing, Luan

Hey, it's me—**LINCOLN LOUD**! With a family this big, remembering all my siblings can be a challenge, especially when everyone's name begins with the letter **L**! But it's not impossible.

   Let me introduce you to my family, and then to the other important people in my life!

Scholastic Inc. 557 Broadway New York, NY 10012 Jefferson City, MO

**LORI** is my oldest sister, and sees herself as the boss. She's mastered the art of the eye roll, and spends her days texting her boyfriend, Bobby (or, as she calls him, Boo-Boo Bear). She literally says "literally" all the time. Lori might get frustrated with me on occasion (read: all the time), but it definitely pays to be nice to her, as she is the only one of us siblings who can drive.

Next in line is my sister **LENI**. She's the local fashionista, and often saves the rest of us from embarrassing fashion faux pas! She's easily distracted and sometimes walks into walls when she's talking—she's not so great at doing two things at once. Although Leni is flighty, she's the sweetest of my sisters and truly has a heart of gold.

Scholastic Inc. 557 Broadway New York, NY 10012 Jefferson City, MO

**LUNA** is the rock star of the family and the third oldest. She's a music fanatic with an encyclopedic knowledge of all things rock and roll—at times she even talks in song lyrics! Luna's energy is usually cranked to a solid 11, and I can always count on her to help out. She'll do almost anything we ask, while also supplying a rocking tune.

Next up is my sister **LUAN**. She is a self-described stand-up comedian who loves bad puns and pulling pranks. She's a really good ventriloquist, too, and can often be found doing comic bits with her dummy, Mr. Coconuts. We're all lucky to have her around (even if her puns sometimes make us groan).

Scholastic Inc. 557 Broadway New York, NY 10012 Jefferson City, MO

**LYNN** is the athlete of the family. For her, it's all sports all the time. Lynn can also turn anything into a game. Need to put away the eggs? Jump shot! Need to clean up the eggs? Slap shot! She's always looking for a teammate, which means the rest of us are fair game for her impromptu dodgeball tournaments or wrestling matches.

If you need a morbid point of view, just talk to my sister **LUCY**. She's obsessed with all things spooky and dark—funerals, vampires, séances, and the like. She's always wearing black, writing moody poetry, and hanging in her "secret dark place." She has a habit of appearing out of nowhere, scaring me every time!

Scholastic Inc. 557 Broadway New York, NY 10012 Jefferson City, MO

**LANA** is the Loud house's resident Ms. Fix-It, and is always ready to lend a hand with repairs. The dirtier the job, the better! Her passions include reptiles, mud pies, and muffler repair. She lives in her overalls and enjoys a handful of kibble from time to time. Other things Lana likes to help with: unclogging the toilet, feeding snakes, and popping back zits.

Whatever Lola wants, Lola gets— or else. **LOLA** is a pageant powerhouse and has the attitude to prove it! Her passions include glitter, photo shoots, and her own beautiful, beautiful face. Lola is the eyes and ears of the household, and as long as we stay on her good side, we've got a fierce ally (and a lifetime of free makeovers).

My sister **LISA** is smarter than all us Louds combined! She spends a lot of time in her lab, creating various explosions. She'll likely grow up to be a rocket scientist or a brain surgeon. Or maybe she'll even take over the world. My sisters and I are Lisa's test subjects, but we're cool with it, since she's always there to help with homework—or point out structural flaws in my pillow forts.

**LILY** is the baby and the official Loud house poop machine. She loves roaming around the halls saying "Poo-poo!" She's a giggly, drooly, diaper-ditching free spirit. But even when Lily is running wild, dropping rancid diaper bombs, or slobbering on the remote, she knows how to steal our hearts.

Scholastic Inc. 557 Broadway New York, NY 10012 Jefferson City, MO

Our **MOM** and **DAD** have one simple rule: Don't call for them unless there's blood or law enforcement involved. They like to let us solve our own problems, which is pretty cool. They trust us to figure out life's challenges, but they're always there if we need them. Mom and Dad are the glue that keeps this loud and large family together. Mom's a dental hygienist (and an aspiring writer), and Dad is the head of IT for a big company (and an aspiring chef). I think they're pretty great parents.

**CLYDE MCBRIDE** is my best friend! We're two peas in a pod, and have pretty much the same taste in movies, comics, TV shows, toys, and stuff like that. Clyde spends a lot of time at my house. He's an only child, so he thinks it's cool to have siblings around to talk to. He also has a major crush on Lori. Being around her makes him talk like a robot. Yuck.

**HOWARD** and **HAROLD** are Clyde's dads, and they were basically born to be parents—the over-protective, helicopter kind. They're attentive and loving, and they support Clyde a thousand percent. They've even helped my sisters and me. Howard is the emotional parent, while Harold is practical. Clyde is lucky to have two awesome dads!

Scholastic Inc. 557 Broadway New York, NY 10012 Jefferson City, MO

was sleep-joking, and Lucy was sleep-sighing. Unlike most nights, however, it didn't bug me. I popped in some earplugs and closed my eyes with a smile, hoping my new spirit friends had a few pairs of earplugs, too.

**12**

The next morning got off to a normal start for a Saturday. Better than normal, actually. I managed to get the TV to myself after breakfast, which meant I could play the new video game Lori had lent me—*Acne Blasters*. You pilot a spaceship through a galaxy of pus-filled planets, blasting them with face wash and zit cream until they explode. Gross, I know—but also oddly satisfying. Charles was sleeping next to me on the couch, oblivious to the loud blasts and explosions on-screen.

I'd made it all the way through the Blackhead Nebula and was about to face the final boss, Admiral Abscess, when I felt a sudden, chilly breeze across the back of my neck. I looked over my shoulder at the front door, but it was closed. *Huh, that's weird.* I returned my attention to the screen, where Admiral Abscess was closing in on my ship.

"Not on my watch!" I shouted, firing a round of super-concentrated zit cream right at his stomach.

Another cold air current swept across the room. This time, it felt strangely familiar. Then it hit me—maybe it was one of the spirits from yesterday, wanting to check out *Acne Blasters,* too!

"Um, hey," I called into the living room. I felt a tiny bit foolish, but then again, none of my sisters was around to hear. "Want to come hang out?"

Suddenly, Charles leapt up and started barking. I yelped, almost dropping the game controller.

"Charles, what the heck?" I asked, trying to keep my eyes on Admiral Abscess—I almost had him! Charles let out a growl. I glanced over and saw him staring intently at the couch cushion next to him, teeth bared and hackles raised.

"Charles, relax," I said. "It's a friendly spirit. It can hang with us!" Charles ignored me and kept barking at the invisible entity.

I heard a triumphant shout and whipped my head back around to look at the TV screen. Admiral Abscess had overtaken my spaceship. I watched helplessly as it sank into a pit of pus.

"Nooo!" I moaned. "I was so close!" I threw the controller aside, frustrated, as Lana came running into the living room.

"Hey, Charles, ready for agility practice? I filled in all those holes in the yard and set up a new course." Charles barked happily and ran over to her. Lana glanced at me. "You guys weren't in the middle of anything, were you?" she asked. I shook my head and waved her away. I wasn't about to tell her about my spirit friend.

Except . . . was it a friend? Why had it made Charles so upset? And why had it made me lose my game?

Then I shook my head. I was being crazy.

It wasn't the spirit's fault that I'd lost; I'd just gotten distracted. I picked up the controller and started the level over. This time, Admiral Abscess was mine.

Later that afternoon, I decided to finally get started on a homework assignment I'd been putting off all quarter—a star chart of the night sky. I locked myself in my room and got down to business, first tracing all the constellations with pencil, then going over them with ink. After hours of work, my wrists were cramped and my vision was blurry, but I was finally down to my last star cluster.

"'Pleiades, also known as the Seven

Sisters,'" I read off my notes as I carefully drew in the stars. "Who was the lucky kid with just seven?" I wondered aloud.

Suddenly, I heard a hoarse, rasping laugh right in my ear. Gah! I jumped and turned around—but no one was there. Maybe I'd imagined it. I'd spent way too long staring at this star chart. But then I heard the voice again—and this time it wasn't laughing. I froze, trying to make out what it was saying.

*"M-m-my room now!"*

My eyes widened. I looked frantically around my room for the source of the voice, but it seemed to be coming from more than one spot. I got up and started searching for hidden speakers or wires, but there was nothing out of place. My eyes fell back on my star chart.

I gasped. It was now completely blank. Where had all my constellations gone?! I'd spent hours drawing them in *pen*!

Outside in the hall, I heard Lori shriek.

I flung open my door and saw her standing at the opposite end of the hallway, staring at a blank piece of paper. When she saw me, she quickly put it behind her back and tried to act casual.

"Lori, what's wrong?" I asked.

"Oh, nothing," she said nervously. I frowned and started to close my door, until I heard her mutter under her breath.

"I'm losing my mind, is all. How could the words just . . . disappear?"

I grabbed my blank star chart and ran out into the hallway.

"Did it happen to you, too? I just spent hours drawing constellations and they all disappeared!" I told her. Lori looked at me, surprised but also relieved.

"Seriously? I thought I was going nuts! I was writing a letter to Bobby—like *hand*writing, literally the most romantic thing ever—when I heard this weird voice. But I was alone in the room!" she said. I nodded, my throat going dry. "And then when I looked back at my letter, everything I'd written was *gone*." She looked embarrassed. Lori doesn't like to admit when she doesn't know what's going on. It's an oldest child thing, I think. "Maybe we both just used a defective pen?" she said uncertainly.

I brightened—that was probably it. I held up my pen, a plain black ballpoint. Lori held up hers, a fancy green gel pen. Okay, so it wasn't that.

"I don't get it. What else could have made my letter disappear?" Lori asked.

I hesitated. If I told her it might be spirits, she'd just laugh at me. But if I showed her Clyde's and my video from yesterday, she'd know that I lied to get her and the rest of my sisters out of the house. Lori stared at me, waiting for an answer. Finally, I just shrugged.

She shook her head. "Whatever. This is what I get for trying to be all old-fashioned and romantic. From here on out, I'm sticking to texts." She tossed the now-blank paper aside, took out her phone, and stomped downstairs.

I glanced back down the hallway toward my bedroom. Were the spirits in there, trying to claim my room for themselves? Is that why they'd made my homework disappear? I frowned and picked up Lori's blank letter. Did they want Lori's room, too? What was going on here?

**T**hat night, my parents went back to Jean Juan's French-Mex Buffet for another round of couples' karaoke. Mom thought Dad's voice might need a break, but he whispered fervently that they had to defend their title.

They left us a pan of Dad's delicious Lynn-sagna. After dinner, we were all standing around the kitchen, fighting over the last bits of crunchy noodles in the dish, when Leni cleared her throat.

"Guys, I don't want to leap to concussions, but did one of you take my sunglasses?" She probably meant "conclusions," but with Leni you can never tell. Instinctively, we all looked at her head—that's usually where her sunglasses are when she can't find them—but they weren't there. Everyone shrugged. Leni sighed. "Oh well, it's probably my fault. I'm always losing things."

Luan turned toward Leni, looking uncharacteristically serious. "Actually, Leni, it's not just you. I can't find Mr. Coconuts," she said, her voice cracking. "I lock him in his trunk every night, but this morning he wasn't there . . . and the trunk was still locked!"

I almost choked on a lasagna noodle. Mr. Coconuts can be pretty annoying, but none of us would ever mess with him—not just because Luan loves him, but also because he has those creepy dummy eyes that seem to follow you around the room.

"Dudes, while we're on the subject of stuff going missing . . . what happened to all the hot water?" piped up Luna. "My shower turned icy this morning, even though I was the first in line for the bathroom."

"This house is ancient. Maybe there's something wrong with the water heater," Lori said, trying to sound nonchalant, though she seemed a little freaked out. Lana, our resident plumber, looked offended.

"Hey, I keep ol' Betty in tip-top shape,"

she said. "There should always be enough hot water for at least five showers." As she and Luna started squabbling, I thought I saw something out of the corner of my eye streaking past the doorway to the darkened dining room. Lola grabbed my sleeve, looking terrified.

"Linky, did you see that, too?" she asked. I nodded, and we darted over to the doorway. I looked into the shadowy dining room and gasped. The grandfather clock was levitating inches off the ground. Before I could say anything, Lola screeched to the others, "Guys! Guys! Come look!"

My sisters ran over to join us just as *SLAM!*—the grandfather clock fell to the floor and started shaking and chiming. Everyone screamed—even Lucy, which I didn't think was even remotely possible.

"Get back, it's not safe!" I yelled, pushing everyone into the kitchen. "Lynn, give me a hand with this table!" Lynn and I flipped the kitchen table on its side, then pushed it against the doorway as a barricade. "That should hold them off for a minute," I panted.

"Lincoln, what the heck is going on?" Lori demanded. I looked at my sisters, trying to think of how to explain the mess I'd gotten us into. Lily toddled over and grabbed my hand, pointing to the refrigerator and her alphabet magnets.

"We can play later, Lilster, but right now I need to—"

"No, Lincoln, look!" Lynn said, slugging me in the arm and also pointing to the fridge.

I gasped in horror as I realized the colorful alphabet letters were moving . . . *by themselves.* The red letter *G* sidled up to the purple *E.*

"Dudes, it's spelling something!" Luna shouted. I watched, frozen, as the letters slid across the fridge to form the words *G-E-T O-U-T.* Everyone gasped.

"It's not safe in here, either," I cried. "Everyone to the garage! I'll explain there."

Lola narrowed her eyes at me. "No, explain *now,*" she insisted. Suddenly, all the magnets fell off the fridge and clattered to the floor. Lola screamed and ran for the back door, diving through the dog flap in a very un-Lola-like fashion. The rest of us scrambled through the regular door and raced to the garage. Lori was the last one out of the house.

She stumbled into the garage, breathing very hard, and immediately locked the door behind her.

"Okay, Lincoln, *now* you're going to explain," she said. I looked around at my sisters—I'd never seen them so scared. Even Lisa, woman of science, was nervous. I took a deep breath.

"I don't know how to explain this, but last night, when you guys were at Flip's, Clyde and I found ghosts in the house," I told them. Lisa rolled her eyes, back to her skeptical self.

"All right, where do I even begin to explain how ludicrous this is," she started, but Luna cut in.

"Come on, Lisa, you can't pretend you haven't been noticing freaky stuff, too. I heard you asking about who knocked over your beakers," she said. Lisa glared at her.

"Look, at first we didn't know what kind of spirits they were. It seemed like they just wanted to throw a little party in the attic," I said. "They were actually pretty cool to hang out with, so . . . I kind of told them they could stay." My sisters looked at me as if I were crazy. I went on anyway, trying to explain what had happened, but leaving out the part about tricking them into going to Flip's. Lynn made a fist.

"So we're just going to let a bunch of dumb ghosts kick us out of our own house?" she said, punching a nearby bag of mulch in frustration.

"No way!" I said. "Don't worry, I'm going to take care of it. Clyde and I are *ARGGH!* cadets. We're trained to deal with spirits." I tried my best to look brave and reassuring. "You guys should be safe in here. I don't think the ghosts are interested in our dingy garage."

"Just our bedrooms and tiaras and stuffed animals," said Lola. "Mr. Sprinkles is in there!" she wailed as I exited the garage.

In the driveway, I took out my walkie-talkie and paged Clyde. "Come in, Cadet Clyde. Over."

He answered immediately.

"Cadet Clyde speaking. I mean, here. Wait, present? No, that's a school thing."

"Clyde, don't worry about the walkie lingo. There's some serious paranormal activity going on at my house right now, and I need your help!" I said.

"Cool! Is it our ghost friends from yesterday, back for another party?" he asked. His excitement turned to concern as I explained how the spirits had been messing with me all day—making me lose the video game, causing Charles to freak out, and making my homework disappear.

"But it's not just me, Clyde. The spirits are after my sisters, too. I think they want us out of our house," I said.

"Wait, back up," Clyde said. "Did you say Lori is in danger?"

"Well, technically we *all* are, but yes—" I started to say.

"I'm on my way!" Clyde shouted. Through the walkie-talkie, I heard him break into a run.

**C**lyde was at my house in a flash, decked out in his *ARGGH!* gear and balancing a plate of snickerdoodles in his bike basket. I ran down the driveway to meet him.

"You made it!"

"I brought these to comfort Lori," he explained, holding up the cookies.

"You can give them to her later—she's keeping safe in the garage with the rest of my sisters. Right now, we've got some angry spirits to deal with," I said, squaring my shoulders and heading toward the house. Clyde hesitated, then ran over to put the cookies by the garage door before joining me again.

"Right behind you, Cadet Lincoln!"

Clyde and I stood on the back steps, peering in through the dog flap. The darkened kitchen was silent again.

"This is where the spirits had been last," I whispered. "But I don't see any signs of them now. Come on." I pushed open the door and tiptoed inside. The kitchen seemed empty, but one glance at my EMF detector told me otherwise. The needle was stuck once more at the highest reading. I showed Clyde.

"They're still here somewhere," I said.

Just then, we heard a familiar sound coming from the living room: it was the same scraping and squelching from last night.

"It's them!" I said.

"To the chimney!" Clyde cried. We broke into a run for the living room, but once we got there, the sounds were already moving upward.

"Scratch that—to the attic!" Clyde said. "Sounds like they're returning to their favorite spot."

"Yeah, well, it's time to show them it's not theirs," I replied. "Let's go!" With a rallying cry, we raced up to the second floor, wrenched down the trapdoor, and charged straight up the attic stairs.

The scene in the attic was complete chaos. Gone was the fun and breezy party atmosphere. The furniture wasn't dancing—it was slamming against the walls and floor. Cold and hot air currents ripped through the attic, whipping the dust into miniature cyclones. The strange little song from yesterday had been replaced with angry voices and bloodcurdling screams.

*"Leeeave . . . ouuur home nowww. . . . Get ouuut."*

I wanted to turn and run back out, but I couldn't. Clyde and I were *ARGGH!* cadets.

If we didn't stop the spirits, who would?

I leapt onto the dress-up trunk and shouted into the chaos, "Hey, spirits!" The trunk started rattling, but I held on tight, refusing to budge. "Who do you think you are, trying to scare my family?"

Clyde jumped up onto the trunk next to me. "Yeah! Tell 'em, Lincoln!"

The furniture kept slamming against the floor, and the lights began to flicker. The angry voices got louder and louder. I shouted with all my might.

"This is our house, too! And if you can't share it with all us Louds, then you can't stay! My sisters may be loud and crazy, but I'd much rather live here with them than with a bunch of jerks like you!"

And just like that, the slamming and

flickering and screaming stopped.

Clyde and I looked at each other. Was it over? Were they gone? I started to breathe a sigh of relief, when I heard a faint, eerie giggle. Clyde and I whipped around—only to see Lola and Lana fall out of a nearby closet.

"What are you guys doing up here? You could have gotten hurt!" I cried, alarmed. But then I heard more giggles, and turned to see the rest of my sisters stepping out from behind furniture, screens, and boxes.

**C**lyde and I looked at each other again, flabbergasted.

"*You guys* are the ghosts? But . . . how?" I asked. "And more importantly, why?"

"Because you were being a huge jerk!" Lola blurted out.

"What Lola *means* is that this is our house,

too, and we thought you might need a reminder of that," Lori said, stepping out from behind the wardrobe. Beside me, Clyde gasped and started stuttering.

"L-L-Lori," he mumbled. Thinking fast, I shoved a beanbag under him just as he passed out.

"Yeah," Lana chimed in. "It didn't take us long to realize what you were up to yesterday, trying to kick us out of every room."

"And then making up the most ridiculous lie ever about Flip's!" Lori added. "I mean, when would he ever give away passes to Dairyland? He's literally the cheapest guy in town."

"But he gave you guys free Flippees," I said defensively. My sisters laughed.

"No he didn't. We just made that up so you would think we'd actually left," Luan explained.

"But . . . but . . . you had the Flippee cup!" I said to Lynn, completely confused.

"I just grabbed an old one from the back of Vanzilla. There were like fifty in there." She shrugged.

"So wait—how did you guys get up to the attic? I never saw you go back inside the house," I said. Lisa proudly explained that she'd applied her new super-adhesive to the bottoms of their shoes, allowing them to scale the chimney and climb in through the attic window.

Ah. That explained the "spirit" sounds in the chimney.

Looking extremely pleased with themselves, my sisters went on to explain how they had created the ghost "party." The rattling trunk was Lori's doing—she'd simply set her phone to vibrate, placed it inside the trunk, then hid and kept calling it until we got to the attic.

"Like I said, this is literally the only place in the house with good reception," she said.

Luna pulled out her guitar and played the strange, otherworldly tune for us.

"I didn't know guitars could sound like that," I admitted.

"I told you, bro, it's my new whammy bar," she said. "If you'd stuck around to jam, I could have shown you."

Lynn explained how she'd made the furniture "levitate" by using the pulleys from her weight machine. Luan told me she'd filled the wardrobe with balloons from her birthday party gigs. Leni stepped forward and proudly demonstrated how she'd used her blow-dryer to create hot and cold air currents.

"Now, when are you going to let me try that fauxhawk?" she asked, eyeing my hair critically.

"Wait a second. What about my EMF detector? It was going crazy," I said, pulling it out of my pocket. "Actually, it still is," I added, confused. Lisa scoffed and grabbed it out of my hand.

"I don't mean to insult your intelligence, elder brother, but there are about a billion household appliances that can set these puppies off," she said, then began rattling off a long list. "Microwaves, dishwashers, electric toothbrushes, clock radios, Dad's karaoke machine—"

"Okay, okay, I get it," I said, taking the detector from her and putting it back in my pocket. "But how did you guys do all that spooky stuff around the house, like when I was playing *Acne Blasters*?" I figured the cold air currents were Leni's doing, but what about Charles freaking out?

Lana grinned. "I told you—Charles can do anything I show him how to do. So I just showed him this!" She got on all fours and started growling at an invisible spot, her teeth bared. Okay, that was pretty convincing. But what about that creepy voice I'd heard in my room, and my disappearing homework? Those definitely couldn't be explained.

Just then, a hoarse rasp called out from the floor below. *"Leeeave . . . my . . . room . . . now!"*

I jumped, then realized that everyone else was giggling and looking at Luan. She took a little bow and explained that she and Mr. Coconuts had spent lots of time working on throwing her voice. I sighed. And here I was almost feeling sorry for that blockhead.

"Well, whoever made my homework disappear? That wasn't cool. I spent hours on that constellation chart."

"Fear not," said Lucy, taking a step forward. "I merely filled your pen with vanishing ink." She held up her own pen and notebook. "It's what I use for all my venting so no one can read it. All you have to do to make it visible again is hold it up to a light." She glanced down at her notebook. "Of course, now that you all know that, I guess I'll have to destroy this."

"But, Lori, you wrote out a letter to Bobby with the vanishing ink, didn't you?" I asked.

Lori shook her head. "No, I just told you I had so you'd be even more creeped out. That was literally a blank piece of paper."

I sighed. At least this meant I didn't have to do my star chart over. I could just hand it in with a flashlight so Mrs. Johnson would be able to read it.

"What about the creepy shadow walking through the dining room?" I tried to think of what else I'd missed.

"Mr. Sprinkles, doing his best runway walk," Lola said, hugging her stuffed bear.

"The moving grandfather clock?" I asked.

"Team effort with Lori's cell phone and my guns," said Lynn, kissing her biceps.

"The fridge magnets?"

"Easily manipulated by a much stronger

magnet across the room," Lisa said. "Though our youngest sibling deserves credit for the idea," she added, patting Lily on the head.

All that was left to explain was the stuff I hadn't seen: Mr. Coconuts's disappearance, the icy shower, the stolen sunglasses . . .

"Oh, no one touched Mr. Coconuts. I'd never let that happen," Luan said.

"And my shower didn't really turn cold," said Luna.

"And I never actually lost my sunglasses," chimed in Leni. Then she stopped, felt the top of her head, and frowned. "Oh wait, I guess I did."

"So you guys just lied to me?" I said, feeling a little hurt.

"Well . . . yeah," Lori said. "Kind of like how you lied to us to try to get us out of the house."

Touché.

"Lincoln, we get that ghost hunting is important to you, but so are the things we want to do around the house," Lori went on. "You can't just expect us to drop what we're doing—or worse, trick us into leaving." The others nodded.

I looked down, ashamed. I couldn't believe how selfish I'd been.

"I'm really sorry, guys. I've been a huge jerk. I don't expect you to forgive me, but—"

"Of course we forgive you, Linky!" Lola interrupted. "Getting to scare the poop out of you more than made up for your jerkiness!"

"Plus, you did just say you'd rather live with us than with those ghosts," added Leni, smiling.

"I meant it," I said, smiling back.

"In the future, just give us a little advance

notice, and we'll be happy to clear out . . . or share our space with you," Lori said.

Behind me, I heard Clyde starting to stir.

"Um, exactly how much advance notice do you need?" I asked her. Lori narrowed her eyes.

"Seriously? You're trying to get rid of me already?"

"No, it's just we have about five seconds before Clyde sees you and passes out again," I said.

"Oh, right," she said. "I'm going, I'm going!"

Later, with Lori gone, I explained to Clyde everything he had missed while he was passed out. He mostly seemed impressed with my sisters' wide range of ghost-faking skills.

"Wow, a cell phone on vibrate. Genius! Lori is just as clever as she is beautiful." Clyde sighed, then added, "You know, I'm actually relieved the spirits didn't turn out to be real. They were way scarier than anything Hunter's had to deal with on *ARGGH!*"

Oh no—*ARGGH!* I looked at Clyde, panicked.

"We can't send in our video. It's all fake!"

"But it's already been submitted." Clyde gasped, horrified. "We sent fraudulent footage to Hunter Spector. He'll strip us of our *ARRGH!* cadet credentials!"

"Maybe they won't put it on the show," I said quickly, trying not to freak out. "I mean, they probably got thousands of submissions."

"Yeah, but none as awesome as ours. Or as awesome as ours would be if it were real.

Which it's not. Which makes us fakes. Frauds! Phonies!" Clyde was spiraling. I grabbed him by the shoulders and came to a decision.

"Look, if they put our video on *ARGGH!,* we'll just have to write to Hunter and let him know it's fake," I said. "They'll probably take away our credentials, but after the past forty-eight hours, I think I'm done with deception." Clyde nodded sadly. We had no other choice.

**A** week later, I was about to leave for Clyde's to watch the newest episode of *ARGGH!* My stomach was in knots. I was dreading the possibility of seeing our video afterward. But as I headed for the door, my sisters called out to me from the living room.

"Lincoln, where are you going? Aren't you

going to watch *ARRGH!* with us?"

I stopped in my tracks. "Wait . . . you guys actually want to watch that show?"

"Of course. We want to see ourselves on TV!"

I shook my head. I sure didn't.

Just then, the doorbell rang. It was Clyde, holding a tub of homemade banana pudding.

"I got Lori's text about watching the show at your house," he said. "But don't worry, I came prepared." He pulled down his night-vision goggles and stumbled inside. I sighed and led him over to the couch. No turning back now.

I'm sure it was a great episode, but I was so nervous about the video spotlight at the end that I could barely concentrate on what was happening. I think Hunter was tracking the spirit of a crazed cruise ship captain or an angry elevator operator, I can't remember. My stomach lurched as he wrapped up the hunt and turned to the camera.

"All right, *ARGGH!* cadets, it's the moment you've all been waiting for—our first-ever Cadet Spotlight!"

"I can't look," I said.

"Put on your goggles," said Clyde, still wearing his.

On-screen, Hunter faced the camera with a serious expression.

"We received thousands of submissions for this first spotlight. Some were bone-chilling. Others were unexpectedly hilarious. And a few were simply . . . masterpieces."

The first still from our video flashed on-screen. My heart sank. My sisters cheered.

"We're famous!" Lola squealed. I covered

my eyes, too ashamed to watch.

Hunter went on. "The next video you're about to see is clearly a creation."

"Wait, what?" I said, looking up. Clyde ripped off his goggles and gaped at the screen.

"And while it may not be real, never have I seen such a beautiful simulation of the work we do. Only true *ARGGH!* cadets could create such a masterful ode to the art of ghost hunting. Cadets Lincoln and Clyde, from Royal Woods, Michigan, my night-vision goggles are off to you."

"And *us!*" added Lynn. "Woo! Roll the tape!"

The video began. I looked at Clyde in disbelief.

"Hunter didn't strip us of our credentials!" I exclaimed.

"He applauded our work!" Clyde cried.

"Don't you mean *our* work?" asked Luan.

As the video played, my sisters proudly pointed out their contributions to the paranormal activity.

"Nice work with those pulleys, Lynn," said Lana.

"Lori, that phone trick is totes genius," said Leni.

"Could you make me a copy of this song, Luna?" asked Lucy. "I've been looking to expand my funeral playlist."

I peered closely at the screen, spotting something in the bottom right corner that I hadn't noticed up in the attic before. The holy grail of paranormal activity: two floating orbs.

"Cool! Which one of you made those?" I asked, pointing to the faint, floating orbs that shimmered in the flickering attic lights. My sisters all exchanged blank looks.

"I didn't," Lori said.

"Neither did I, dude," added Luna.

"Even if I possessed the proper equipment to generate a hologram, those orbs appear to be composed of something else entirely," Lisa mused. My sisters grew silent, staring at the screen in confusion. Clyde and I looked at each other, eyebrows raised, then leapt up from the couch at the same time, knocking over the pudding.

"You ready to do this again, Cadet Clyde?" I exclaimed.

"You know it, Cadet Lincoln!" He grinned and grabbed his video camera.

"Time to get our ghost!"

SNEAK
PEEK!

ARCADE
OR BUST!

BY
AMARIS GLASS

**"L**incoln, can you hold Hops while I clean out his cage?"

"Lincoln, I need you to teach me how to Hula-Hoop."

"Lincoln, will you help me polish my coffins?"

Sisters. They all want a piece of you.

Picture this: I'm Lincoln Loud, minding

my own business in my linen-closet-turned-bedroom, doing a little dance in my undies because it's Saturday.

But not just any old regular no-big-deal-nothing-to-do Saturday. Today was the most exciting Saturday in the history of weekends! I had freedom (my parents were away all day at a seminar on singing to your houseplants to help them grow). I had quarters (Captain Coinbottom, my piggybank, was practically too heavy to carry). And I had a quest: be the first in line with Clyde at the arcade to play *Marshmallow Martian Blasters.*

What's *Marshmallow Martian Blasters,* you ask? It's only the most legendary, full-size, never-been-played-before video game known to kid-kind. It was one of the first games to appear in arcades when our parents were in grade school. *No kid living* has ever seen it in real life. Like Bigfoot.

Only, we've managed to find it!

And it's coming to Gus' Games N' Grub.

"Lincoln!" Luna pounded on my door, interrupting my undies dance. "Project Day meeting in five minutes!"

No.

NO.

*Nooooooo.*

Not Project Day. Not today!

I flopped down on my bed and groaned into my pillow. This ruined *everything*. Why did Lori have to invent this miserable tradition, anyway?

Project Day is just what it sounds like: a day

full of projects. In a house with eleven kids, two parents, four pets, and one Vanzilla, someone is always trying to get something done. Usually several someones, and they all need help.

I admit, Project Day can be pretty handy when you want to build a bike ramp in the backyard but can't do it by yourself. In a family this size, there's always someone with the skills you need to get your project done. Everyone helps everyone, knowing that the next time Project Day rolls around, the favor will be returned.

Like I said, it's not a bad deal—unless you already have plans. *Big* plans. Important plans. Intergalactically pivotal plans! Why todaaaayyyyy? *Whyyyyyyyy?*

"Lincoln—er, Firesticks! Are you there?

Come in, Firesticks!" Clyde's voice crackled from my walkie-talkie. "Are you ready for Operation Be First in Line to Play *Marshmallow Martian Blasters* and Get the High Score? Over."

I stretched my leg out and grabbed the walkie with my toes—a skill I spent one very bored week last summer perfecting while all my sisters were sick—and pressed the button to talk to Clyde.

"I'm here, but I have bad news, buddy." I took a deep breath. "Lori's decided—"

"That she's done with old Too-Tall McSkinnyPants and is in the market for someone new?" I could practically hear Clyde smoothing his hair.

"*Clyde!* Focus! It's bad." I slid down to the

floor. "She's instituting Project Day. Today."

"No."

"Yes."

*"No."*

*"Yes."*

"Lincoln, this ruins *everything*!"

"I know! What am I going to do?"

More pounding on my door, this time from Lola. "You better be getting dressed, Lincoln. No one wants to see you in your underwear!"

"Clyde, they're coming for me. How do I get out of this?" I jumped up and began stuffing my backpack with clothes, comics, and my secret stash of fruit leather. The situation was dire. I might have to run away.

"Lincoln, this is bad. Over."

"I know."

"Like, *really* bad. Over. Project Days can last forever! Over."

"I *know*! Clyde, you're not helping. Over."

"Sorry. Okay, let's just take a minute to breathe. . . ." I could hear Clyde inhaling and exhaling so deep *I* was getting dizzy. "Of course! We need an Operation."

*Right.* "A *new* Operation," I said.

"A Get Out of Project Day Operation."

"A Get Out of Project Day Without Making Everyone Mad Operation."

"A Divert and Distract Escape Operation?" asked Clyde.

I considered it. That had worked well for me in the past, but . . . "No, I think more of a Fool My Sisters and Then Walk Merrily Away Operation."

"Ah, a Help with Project Day Without Actually Helping Operation. Classic."

"A Be Really Eager but Absolutely Useless So No One Will Want My Help and I Can Sneak Away Without Anyone Knowing What I'm Really Up To Operation."

"Lincoln, that's genius!"

It really was. "And I haven't even gotten to the best part. Every Project Day has a Floater, and if I can convince everyone to pick me, I won't be tied to one certain project. I'll float around, and no one will know where I'm supposed to be. When I disappear, no one will even know I'm gone. *Poof!*"

"Whoa . . . you're an inspiration. I'm proud to call you my best friend."

"Thanks, Clyde. Me too." Part of me knew

that didn't even make sense, but I was so impressed with myself I let it slide and did a somersault off the bed, landing in a gloriously awkward heap that did nothing to dampen my enthusiasm. "This is totally going to work. *Marshmallow Martian Blasters,* here we come!"

Lori and Leni's room was full of sisters and chatter as I raced inside and hurled myself onto Leni's bed. "Hey, guys! Happy Project Day!"

Everyone stopped and stared at me. Lola reached over and touched my forehead. "Do you have a fever? Why are you being weird?"

I batted her hand away and grinned at

everyone. "Who's being weird? I'm just excited!"

Lori sighed. "Whatever, Lincoln. We have a busy day ahead of us, so let's get started."

Everyone shrugged and went back to what they were doing. Except Lucy. She was still watching me.

Or maybe she wasn't. It was hard to tell under all those bangs. I pretended to pick my nose, just to see if she was watching me or not.

Lucy made a face. "Gross, Lincoln."

*Whoops.* Guess she was.

Lori pounded her shoe on the dresser like a judge with a gavel. "Project Day meeting will now come to order. First order of business: The Listing of The Projects. Coin toss to decide which sequence we go in." She pointed her shoe around the room. "Who has a coin?"

I hastily fished a quarter out of my pocket—courtesy of Captain Coinbottom's bottom—and tossed it to her. "Here, it's on me."

Lori caught the quarter and looked at it, then over at me. "Thanks. Wait, are you sure you're not up to something? You're being awfully helpful."

"That's because I'm a helpful guy!"

## TO BE CONTINUED . . .